ON YOUR MARK, GET SET, HOP!

D1621915

F. WARNE & Co

One summer day, Peter, Benjamin, and Lily were collecting fresh strawberries from Mr. Tod's garden.

The rabbits knew it was risky.

But they couldn't resist!

Suddenly, Peter heard rustling in the strawberry patch . . .

"Mr. Tod!" gasped Peter.

"Hello, my floppy-eared friends," said the fox, licking his lips.

"Oh, this is bad. This is really bad!"

Benjamin said.

"I'm in the mood for some fun and games today."

Mr. Tod chuckled.
"If you complete my challenges, I'll let you have my perfectly ripe strawberries. If you fail, then I'll have you all for dinner!"

Peter stepped forward. "We're the fittest rabbits in the woods and can complete any challenge.

Bring it on!"

"Here are your challenges,"
said the fearsome fox.

"One: Collect carrots from
Mr. McGregor's garden.

Two: Bring back blackberries
from the Deep Dark Woods.

Three: Nab some nuts from Old Brown's island.
ALL the challenges must be completed by . . .
SUNDOWN."

Peter looked at his friends.
"What are we waiting for?
Let's hop to it!"

Soon, Peter, Lily, and Benjamin arrived at Mr. McGregor's garden. Peter spotted a log leaning up against the high wall and raced up it.

"Up here!" he called.

Benjamin looked up. "Um, it's a very long way to the top!" he said. "What if I skip this challenge?"

"Come on, Benjamin," Lily said. "You are as strong as we are. Hop to it!"

Benjamin took a deep breath and bounded up the log.

"Good job, everyone," Peter said once they were in the garden. He quickly grabbed some carrots and put them in his bag. Suddenly, they heard a loud MEOW.

It was Mr. McGregor's cat.

"Let's get out of here!"

Lily cried.

After running a long way, the rabbits stopped to catch their breaths. They had made it all the way to the Deep Dark Woods.

"Look! Blackberries!"
Lily cried. She stashed
some in her pocket.

"Challenge number two complete!"
Benjamin said.

"Now we need to get to Old
Brown's island," said Peter.
"Let's go!"

"Nutkin, we need your help!"

Peter cried, as the friends arrived at the lake.

"We have to collect some nuts from Old Brown's island," Lily explained. "Will you take us there?"

"Happy to help,"

Nutkin said. "Hop on!"

Rumble, rumble, grumble!

"What was that?" Lily asked.
"It's my tummy," said Benjamin.
"I'm starving! All this running and
rowing is hard work."

"Here," Lily said, pulling a handful of
blackberries from her pocket. "Let's
all have a snack."
The friends munched on the
yummy berries.

"Thanks, Lily,"
said Benjamin.
"My tummy feels
much better!"

Once they reached the island, Nutkin began to look for the stash of hazelnuts. But he didn't get very far before. . . "Run!" cried Peter.

"We've got company!"

It was Old Brown. The grumpy owl didn't want to share any nuts! He swooped down toward the rabbits and Squirrel Nutkin.

"Quick, in here!" Peter yelled.

The friends dived after Peter into a hollow log.

"Tailfeathers!"

squawked Old Brown grumpily,

swooping away to his tree.

"Wait a minute," said Nutkin. "Here's my secret stash of hazelnuts! Nicely done, friends."

Lily scooped up a handful and put them in her pocket with the blackberries.

The challenges were complete!

The rabbits and Nutkin headed back to the raft, and home. Then, the bunnies waved good-bye to Nutkin.

"Thanks for your help," said Lily.

"Come on," said Peter. "We've got some

STRAWBERRIES
to collect!"

The rabbits raced back to Mr. Tod's garden.

Mr. Tod was waiting for them outside his lair.

"We've completed all your challenges!"

declared Peter, showing him the carrots, blackberries,
and nuts they had collected.

"Now we'd like to collect some strawberries,"
said Lily.

But Mr. Tod just laughed nastily.

"You fluffy-eared fools," he said. "You didn't really think I'd let you GO, did you? These will make an excellent side salad for my main course . . .

RABBIT STEW!"

But as the fearsome fox sprang toward them, the bunnies hopped out of his grasp. All the excercise and healthy berries had given them extra

BOUNCE!

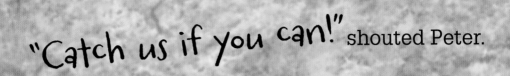

"Catch us if you can!" shouted Peter.

The friends dashed through Mr. Tod's strawberry patch, collecting juicy berries as they went, before escaping into the woods.

"Hmm, these strawberries are SO delicious," said Benjamin happily, as the rabbits shared their prize.

"Delicious and healthy!" Lily agreed. "That's a fact!"